The Lost Goddess

Billie Potter

ISBN:
ISBN-13:
9781072801597

My name is

female   male

A		J		T	
B		K		U	
C		L		V	
D		M		W	
E		N		X	
F		O		Y	
G		P		Z	
H		Q			
I		R			
		S			

DEDICATION

To my Family, Alan and History.

CONTENTS

The Lost Goddess
1.

The pyramids had always been on their skyline. Ever since they could remember, these kids, living in an old Egyptian town, had always been able to see them, they were part of their daily lives.

The pyramids had been there when their parents were young, when their grandparents had been kids and they had been there for well over four thousand years. They had been built by the Pharaohs of ancient Egypt and that was a long time ago, a very long time ago indeed.

Kepri and Jabari were twins, not identical twins, well they couldn't be, Kepri was a girl and Jabari was her brother, a boy, but they were twins.

Kepri and Jabari spent most of their time together, they had been inseparable since birth and had grown up together. They liked the same things, they disliked the same things and they often finished one another's sentences, seeming to know what their twin was thinking or about to say. They liked each other just the same as they liked themselves, they were like one single person.

Where Kepri and Jabari lived the schools started early in the morning and finished before lunch time leaving the children free for the afternoon.

The twins, like a lot of their friends, spent much of their spare time near and around the pyramids.

Often in the afternoons and at the weekends Kepri and Jabari could be found selling all sorts of things to the tourists who visited the pyramids. Many of the local families were not well off, in fact most were poor and so any extra money which could be made was welcome and helped the whole family to get by.

Some of the twin's friends liked to cheat the tourists if they could to get extra money, but Kepri and Jabari were not like that, they liked to be fair, to treat their tourists properly, honestly.

Kepri and Jabari would buy or find all sorts of things which they thought the tourists would like and then sell whatever they had to them. Sometimes it would be hats to protect the visitors from the sun or fans so that they could waft air in their faces to keep cool, sometimes it would be little trinkets for mementoes.

Amongst the favourite things which Kepri and Jabari liked to sell were maps of the area and of the pyramids, they also liked to get printed guides that told the tourists all about the pyramids and the history of Egypt.

The twins had learned all about the area and would offer to take visitors on a guided tour of their own, and to tell them all about the pyramids. They were very clever children and very proud of their pyramids.

The twins really knew their way around the pyramids and the area around them. It had been their playground ever since they were very young. This knowledge came in very useful when they were showing tourists around, but it was even more useful after the tourists had gone and after the officials had locked the gates and closed the site for the day.

Kepri and Jabari seemed to know lots of ways to get past the gates and doors so that they could get back into the pyramid area themselves. They really knew their way around and loved to play and explore when no one else was around.

At school Kepri and Jabari had learned about the pyramids and about ancient Egypt in their history lessons. They especially liked learning about hieroglyphics, that is a sort of picture writing where picture drawings are used to make up words, and the twins had found that they could use them as a sort of secret code so that they could pass secret notes to each other using the hieroglyphics.

They first learned how to write their names, so Kepri looked like; ⌇⌇⌇⌇⌇⌇ and Jabari; ⌇⌇⌇⌇⌇⌇ and they later learned how to make sentences. They learned how some pictures meant different things such as a 'cobra', a kind of snake, sometimes meant 'goddess' or a crocodile actually meant a 'crocodile'.

The twins loved the ancient writing so much and the stories of ancient Egypt that they took time to find books about it, or to visit the little museum in their town which had all sorts of things from the olden days in it.

In the area there were a number of pyramids, but the one that Kepri and Jabari liked the most was a very small plain one which was a little way from all of the other pyramids. Perhaps that is why they liked it, or perhaps it was because they found a small passageway about half way up one side of it which they could get into.

It was not a very long passageway, in fact it was short enough to let the daylight in all the way to the end of it.

At the end of the passageway was a big stone which blocked the end of it. It had some hieroglyphics on it, but some of them had been chiselled off so that it was difficult to make much sense of it, but they had tried and liked to go back time and again to try to work out what it said.

One of the clever things about the Pharaohs and their buildings was that they often built in something special.

The twins had discovered that on one day of the year, in the late afternoon, the sun would shine down their pyramids passageway all the way to the big stone at the end of it and light it up as if it had a big light shining on it.

Kepri and Jabari thought that this was very clever and often wondered how and why it had been done and if it meant anything special.

Today, like any other day, the twins had spent the afternoon trying to sell things to the tourists and trying to help them enjoy their visit to the pyramids.

After the area had been closed for the day the twins made their way to their favourite pyramid, and by chance this was the day when the sun shone all the way down the passageway and onto the inscription stone.

When the twins got there the passageway was in its full glory, it was almost like it was made of gleaming gold and the light seemed to bounce right back out at them.

They rushed to the end of the passageway and sat on the floor resting their backs against the stone and looking back out of the pyramid and towards the sun.

It felt really great, the sun had warmed the inscription stone which they were leant against and somehow today it felt very comfortable, very soft and gentle, they both felt very peaceful and happy.

It was after a few moments that they both realised that something was happening. They looked at each other and clasped each other's hand.

It was a strange feeling, not scary or anything bad, just strange. It seemed as if they were melting into the inscription stone which they were leaning against. In fact, as they looked around, they were sort of melting into the stone, they were gradually disappearing into it and becoming part of it.

Before very long the twins had completely disappeared without a trace.

2.

Softly, gently, slowly the children emerged,
sort of, melted out of the stone. They were
not frightened or upset in any way,
everything felt O.K. felt 'normal'.

Kepri and Jabari were not however back in
the passageway, they were in a really big
hall of some sort. It had big columns or
pillars which seemed to go right up to the
sky. In fact, when the twins looked up, it
seemed that the sky was indeed being held
up by the pillars.

The pillars were very white, very smooth,
there didn't seem to be a joint in them
anywhere. They looked to be one piece of
…… the twins were not sure what they were
made of, … it didn't seem cold like stone
but they seemed very solid.

The floor was also white and the twins
couldn't figure out what they were made of
either, not tiles, not stone block in fact

nothing that they had ever come across before, but again there were no joints in the floor, just smooth, but not cold, just comfortable, in fact everything in this vast hall seemed somehow comfortable, and, ….. well, ….. as if it had grown into whatever it was, into this hall.

It was very light and warm in the hall, very comfortable, very peaceful and they felt somehow quite at home.

It was sometime before Kepri and Jabari noticed the figure stood in front of them, which is surprising because this figure was big, very big. He announced himself as 'ANUBIS' and instructed them to follow him.

The twins knew that 'ANUBIS' was the name of one of Egypt's ancient gods, but they didn't think that this figure could be him. The god ANUBIS was supposed to have the head of a jackal, a sort of dog or wolf, but this ANUBIS didn't. He was big though, much bigger than any grown up the twins had ever seen. He seemed to be important so they did as he had said and followed him, occasionally looking at each other for reassurance, and holding each other's hand.

After following ANUBIS for some time through massive buildings the twins were eventually presented to a seated woman. Again, like ANUBIS, she was bigger than anyone the twins had ever seen before. ANUBIS announced to the children that this was MA'AT and he informed MA'AT that the children were Kepri and Jabari. The twins were astonished that he knew their names as he had not asked them and they had not told him, but he said it as if he had always known who they were.

MA'AT looked at Kepri and Jabari for some time, it felt as if she was looking right into them, right inside them.

Eventually she said to them "You are not dead are you?"

This took the twins by surprise, of all the questions they might have expected, that was not one of them. They eventually managed to say "no" as far as they knew "they were still alive", and MA'AT smiled at them.

"I'm not used to dealing with live people from your world" she explained, "I only ever judge the spirit of the dead".

The children were not expecting that either.

MA'AT explained that back in ancient Egypt when Pharaohs died their soul or spirit was brought before her and she judged whether they had been good enough in their life to be allowed into eternal life in their 'hereafter'. She usually did that by weighing all of their deeds, everything they had done against the 'feather of justice', and if their deeds in life were too bad then they could not pass.

MA'AT looked at Kapri and Jabari and smiled again. She could see right into them and she knew that they were good people, and also that she liked them.

"Why are you here?" MA'AT was asking questions again.

The children didn't know what to say.

"No humans come here without a reason".

MA'AT explained that it was a very long time in human terms since anyone had come before her, and there must be a reason why the twins were here now.

It was only then that Kepri and Jabari realised that they didn't know where they were.

When they started to think about it, this whole place was a bit strange. How did ANUBIS know their names? How did he know they had arrived there? And why did he collect them and take them to MA'AT? What was this place?

MA'AT could see by looking at them all of the questions that were going through the twins minds and so she beckoned them to come and sit with her.

MA'AT, Kepri and Jabari sat together looking a bit like a mother and her children.

The twins had lots of questions about where they were, but MA'AT also had questions she wanted to ask them.

MA'AT got her questions in first, and she asked them if they knew how they had come into this world, the world of MA'AT and ANUBIS and all the others there.

The twins had difficulty answering her questions, they didn't know why they were there, they just were, they only knew that they had been leaning against the inscription stone in their pyramid when they, sort of, melted into it and then came out into this world, the world of MA'AT and ANUBIS.

MA'AT beckoned someone over to her and they had what seemed to be a conversation, least ways the twins thought that it was a conversation. MA'AT and the other person made noises to one another, not noises that made any sense to Kapri or Jabari, but it seemed like some sort of strange language.

"That was THOTH", MA'AT told the twins, he has gone to see if he can find out where, how and why you came into our world.

Now it was the twins turn to ask some questions, and the first on was "Where are we?"

MA'AT smiled at them and thought for a while.

Eventually she told them that somehow they had entered her world, then tried to explain that the world that they, the twins live in, was different to her world, the one they had entered.

MA'AT told them that the two worlds were very different, but sort of side by side, or even perhaps in the same space.

This didn't really help Kepri or Jabari to understand and they asked MA'AT that if these two worlds were in the same space "how come we can't usually see the other world?"

"There are many things that we cannot see" MA'AT said "but that doesn't mean that they are not there". She thought for a while, and then gave the twins an example.

"Do you have torches at home?" she asked, and the twins said that they did.

"Well" said MA'AT, "if you go into a dark room and switch your torch on you can see the beam of light, can't you?"

The twins nodded in agreement.

"Now" asked MA'AT "if you take your torch out into the bright sunlight and switch it on you can't see the beam can you?"

Again the twins nodded in agreement.

"But the beam of light is still there".

The twins, sort of, understood what MA'AT meant so asked how they had crossed into her world and that of ANUBIS and THOTH.

MA'AT said that she didn't yet know except that they had passed through a 'portal' between the two worlds.

The twins asked, with a bit of anxiety, if they would be able to get back.

MA'AT reassured them that they would be able to, and they relaxed a little.

The next question was, again, with regard to their crossing over. "We seemed to go into a big stone and then out again to get here" they said "but you can't go through a stone or rock, its solid."

Again MA'AT thought before she explained to them. "You may be surprised" she said "nothing is as solid as you think".

The children looked at MA'AT and wondered how she might explain this.

She told them that even they were not solid, and followed this by saying that when things get hot, very hot, perhaps when they run around playing, chasing each other, they can see sweat appear on their skin. "Well, that has gone through your skin, so your skin must have holes in it, mustn't, it?"

The twins had to admit that she was right again. They thought she must be very wise.

After a while Kepri and Jabari said to MA'AT that when they did history at school they were told that in ancient Egypt there were gods and goddesses with names such as ANUBIS and THOTH as well as her name, MA'AT, then Kepri and Jabari asked if she and the others were in fact 'gods'.

MA'AT had wondered how long it would be before that question was asked.

"Well" she said, " when the ancient Egyptian Pharaohs and priests first made contact with us they thought we must be gods because we knew much more than they did, and because we gave them advice and information to help them. It was the ancient Egyptian Pharaohs and priests who called us gods. We don't really think of ourselves in that way, we're just us."

"So, how long have you been here?" Kepri asked.

"We don't really have 'time' here" replied

MA'AT, "so there is no answer to that question".

Kepri and Jabari looked at MA'AT wondering what she meant.

MA'AT could see that they were confused so she tried to explain the differences between their two worlds.

"In your world you have day and night, you count that as time and say that seven of them makes a week. Then you watch your moon change its position in your sky and call it a month, and the sun and your seasons, which you call a year, all this is your 'time'."

"We here" said MA'AT "do not have 'time', we live in permanent light, we don't have day and night like you, and we don't have seasons or years, we just have 'now' and 'events'."

Kepri again asked "How do you know how old you are?"

"We don't have age" replied MA'AT, unlike your world, we continue to 'exist', we don't get older."

MA'AT thought for a while and then added "when we interact with your world we use your human generations to help you understand. You two are one generation, then your mum and dad are another generation, as are their parents and so on backwards in 'time'. I think you work out about four generations are equal to one hundred of your years."

THOTH appeared which ended the conversation which the twins and MA'AT were having.

MA'AT and THOTH then had another conversation in their language, which made no sense to either Kapri or Jabari.

It seemed to be a long conversation with what seemed to the twins like lots of questions and answers between MA'AT and THOTH and with lots of movement and excitement between them.

Eventually the conversation came to an end and MA'AT turned around to the twins again.

"I need to ask you some more questions so that we can help you, and also as you may be able to help us" MA'AT said.

The twins nodded and waited for MA'ATs questions.

She started by saying that THOTH had found the place where they had crossed from their world to this one, and asked if they could tell her about the other side of their 'portal'.

Both Kepri and Jabari smiled and told her that it was their favourite place. They told her about the pyramid, far away from all the others, and smaller. Then they said about the passageway in the pyramid and how the sun shone down it on just one moment each

year, and how that had just happened and
how they were leant against the inscription
stone at the end of the passageway which
they 'melted' into and then out into this, her
world.

MA'AT was very interested in the stone that
they had come through and asked them
many questions about it.

The twins told MA'AT as much as they
could. It was a stone that always made them
feel happy and they often just sat there leant
against it because of that. They also told her
about the hieroglyphics that were carved on
it and how they had managed to read some
of what it said.

MA'AT was very interested in this
information. She was told by the children
that the hieroglyphics mentioned festivals
and dancing troupes and acrobats and some
kind of celebration.

MA'AT asked them if it had any names on it
but the twins told her that some of the
inscription had been damaged, had been

chiselled off and they thought that any names that might have been there must have been destroyed.

MA'ATs face dropped at this news, she seemed to become unhappy but she tried to smile and asked the children if they were willing to help if they were able to.

Kepri and Jabari readily agreed to do whatever they could.

3.

MA'AT called for ANUBIS to take the twins back to the portal so that they could return to their world. She had asked them to go back to their side, their world, and look to see if they could find any sign of a name on or near the inscription stone which they crossed through, and to come back when they could report anything which they had found.

And so Kepri and Jabari returned to their own world, and when they crossed back it was as if no time had passed there while they had been gone.

It was a few days before the twins had an opportunity to visit their pyramid, and they took torches with them just in case they would be of help. They also took note pads and pencils so that they could copy anything that might be of interest.

Together the twins looked over the inscription stone. They looked over it many times trying to find clues, to see if there was a name, and if they could find anything that might help.

After a lot of searching and trying to read the stone they both agreed that there was one or two places where the hieroglyphs had been destroyed that were probably, almost certainly names or perhaps just one name. They got their note pads out and drew the outlines of odd bits of carving that were left. One bit they thought was significant because it was part of a female seated and they were pretty sure that it was a hieroglyph meaning 'woman' or perhaps even 'goddess'. They also made a note of how much writing was destroyed either side of this bit of hieroglyph.

They drew;

They included the part of the hieroglyph
which they thought might be the letter 'S'
which hadn't completely been destroyed and
the little bit in front of the seated lady which
they weren't sure about. That was just about
all that they found that might be useful.

This hunt for a name had been both
exhausting and exiting. They were both
feeling happy and a little tired so they leaned
back onto the inscription stone for a rest
and, as before, they melted into it and then
out again into the other world where
ANUBIS was waiting for them.

Almost before the twins had time to think
they were with MA'AT again and she was

looking at them expectantly.

They handed her the drawing that they had just made, hoping it would be useful.

MA'AT looked at it for a while and asked if the hieroglyph was on the inscription stone that they had told her about. The twins confirmed that it was.

MA'AT looked at their drawing for some time and pondered what to say to them. Finally she decided.

"I need to tell you something that happened about 135 of your generations ago" MA'AT said.

"But we don't know the entire story" she continued.

"One of our people crossed over into your world to take a message to your Pharoah, she was followed by another from here".

 MA'AT paused for a while, she seemed to be searching her memory before continuing, "The second one returned but the first never has, and we are sure that she, the second one, did something that has stopped the first from returning to us".

MA'AT again paused while she decided what else to say.

The twins asked what the name of these two were and MA'AT said that she would have to call the second one 'she who's name cannot be spoken in words' as it was impossible for humans to pronounce her name, but she also said that it could be written in hieroglyphics and had THOTH write it out for them.

It looked like this;

MA'AT told Kepri and Jabari that they had asked the second one what had happened in the other world but she refused to answer, she just smiled back at them. Everyone was sure that she had done something but she would not tell them anything.

Kepri and Jabari asked what the first lady was called.

"Ah", said MA'AT, she paused and thought for a moment, "This is a problem. We wish we could tell you, but because her name has been destroyed in your world we are unable to give her or speak her name". MA'AT sighed and looked sad.

"If a name is destroyed, obliterated, then that person may stop existing, that is why we need you to try to find her name for us, so that she can exist and so that she can return to us".

MA'AT looked right into the eyes of Kepri and Jabari and with a plea in her voice asked "Will you help to find her name for us?"

The twins solemnly agreed to try their best to find this missing name. Then they were returned once more to their world with the help of ANUBIS.

Kepri and Jabari were both exited with their new task but also a little daunted at the responsibility that was now upon their shoulders.

If they could find the 'name' then they would have helped, even made it possible for this person, this female, this goddess from the other world to exist. But, if they failed! ………………..

The twins talked together for hours, they planned what to do, talked about where they might find the hieroglyphic name that they were hunting, and they talked about how they might recognise it if they saw it.

They had a piece of the name, the bit that was in the middle of the name, the seated lady and possibly the letter 'S' and a couple of 'picture' bits in front of the seated lady. They knew how much had been chiselled away before and after the piece they had and so they felt that they knew roughly how long the name might be, that information should help.

Kepri and Jabari made a list of places where they might find the hieroglyphics and decided on a plan to visit places and to look in books which might help.

They had been wandering around their local museum for hours, making notes in their note books and sometimes drawing things.

The twins noticed a pot, well, not a complete pot, it was broken and although it had been pieced back together, there were bits missing. However, it had an inscription on it, and although most of the inscription was missing, they noticed that a bit that was there had a bit of the picture that was the same as their hieroglyph, so they drew it;

They knew that it may have nothing to do with their 'name', but it was worth making a note, just in case.

There was also a piece of papyrus, just a corner of one, which had a hieroglyph on it of the picture word for 'woman' or 'goddess'. It didn't have the 'S' after it, just a seated lady followed by a downward slash. They drew it in their book just in case it was of use later.

It looked like this;

That was all that the museum had which they thought might be of use.

For probably the first time in their lives the twins did not rush out of school when it finished. Instead they asked their teacher if it would be O.K. to look at some of the books in the school library.

Kepri and Jabari knew, because of their history lessons, that there were books about ancient Egypt, and they would have pictures in them of hieroglyphic writing and photographs of old inscriptions from temples and tombs, so there might be something to help them in their quest.

Together the twins looked through many books. They didn't find anything of use on this day and so they decided to stay behind every day until they had looked at every book.

Several days later their eyes were beginning to sting because of looking so carefully at all of the pictures. Other children would have given up long ago, but Kepri and Jabari were not 'other children', even though their eyes hurt they kept looking.

The next book they looked at was about some parts of religion in ancient Egypt and included all sorts of rituals. It seemed like a book of fun to the twins as it told of how the ancients danced and celebrated on special occasions. Importantly, it talked about the goddess of these festivities. She seemed like a happy, cheerful goddess, she liked to have fun.

Unfortunately the book said that her name had been lost thousands of years ago because a Pharaoh didn't think there should be so much enjoyment on religious occasions.

There was one bit of the name left on a tablet that had survived, although much of it had been damaged,

so the twins drew what was left;

and they hoped that this would be of use to them.

It had been more than a week that the twins had stayed behind at school to look through the books and that meant that they had not been able to go to the pyramid site and sell things to the tourists. This made a difference to the whole family finances, so they decided that they had better get back to doing that for a while.

The thing that they liked best with tourists was when they could persuade them to be taken on a guided tour.

The twins had an unusual request from a couple of tourists. The tourists had read that the ancient workers who built the pyramids lived in a specially made village close by, and the ruins were still there, so could they look at these ruins?

Kepri and Jabari knew the ancient village ruins because they and their friends often played there. It was good for hiding or jumping out to surprise one another. So the twins took their tourists to the village.

The tourists were impressed with the tour that the twins were giving them, they really did know lots about the village.

Kepri and Jabari took the tourists to various ruined houses which they thought might be of interest. They pointed out writings by side of door entrances which the ancient inhabitants must have had painted on, sometimes for good luck sometimes to give a name to their home. In some houses there were little shrines where the ancient workers would have made offerings to their favourite 'god', and there were all sorts of interesting things that the twins showed the tourists which gave an insight to how they lived in ancient times.

It was next to one of the shrines that both Kepri and Jabari noticed a little bit of painted hieroglyphic which might have something to do with their search, so as soon as they had said goodbye to the tourists they rushed back to the ruined village.

Sure enough, on closer inspection, there was some hieroglyphic painted symbols,

 it was;

and looked as if it might just join up with one of the drawings which they had previously recorded.

After they had drawn this hieroglyph in their note book they searched around to see if they could find any more and luckily for them they found, hidden behind a stone, another part of it which was;

so they made a drawing of that to.

It had been a few weeks since they had visited MA'AT in the other world.

The twins decided to put together the bits of drawings that they had so far made to see if it made sense. Not all of their drawings fitted, but the ones that did made up something that looked as if it fitted together,

it was;

There were still bits missing and they knew that it wasn't complete, but they drew up what they thought it might be with the missing bits filled in as best they could guess,

it looked like;

Neither Kepri or Jabari were sure what to make of it, or if it would be enough to help

MA'AT, and they wondered what to do next.

They decided to ask their teacher about it, but without saying what they were up to or why they were doing it, they would just say that it was a project they were working on.

Their teacher was not surprised at their request, he knew that they were clever children and that they were working on something, so he readily agreed to try to interpret their hieroglyphics.

He told them that it was undoubtable incomplete, that it was just the first part of a name. It was a queen or goddess and the first part was a description of her. He told them that he thought that hieroglyphics said that she had 'something', perhaps 'golden' hair, and 'green' or 'turquoise' possibly 'eyes' and a complexion of cream, and that her name very probably started with the letter 'S', but that was as much as he could tell them.

Kapri and Jabari decided to take their findings back to MA'AT as they couldn't find any more of the name.

ANUBIS was waiting exactly where he had been when they last crossed back from the other world. He took them straight to MA'AT.

MA'AT looked at the children's sketch of the hieroglyph that they had managed to piece together, and she smiled a little.

"That certainly is who we are looking to find" she told them, "she has golden hair, eyes of green and her complexion is that of cream, but the name is still missing". She went on, "and without the name we cannot help her to come back into existence".

Everyone was a little sad, they knew that Kepri and Jabari had tried their best, and they were so close, but there were letters missing and a name cannot be guessed, it has to be certain.

The twins, with heavy hearts, promised to try again, but said that they really had tried everything they could. ANUBIS took them back to their 'portal' to return to their world.

As they emerged from the inscription stone in the passageway, in their favourite pyramid Jabari dropped his torch. As it hit the floor it switched itself on and a beam of light shone against the bottom of the inscription stone.

They both saw the same thing at the same time. There was a slight gap underneath it, underneath the inscription stone, not a big gap, perhaps only the width of a finger, but it was definitely there. They tried to look under it to see what if anything there was to see, but they couldn't get their faces low enough to the floor.

Jabari found a twig laying not far away and sort of brushed it in the gap. He could feel something, and there was a scraping sound. After a few attempts all that came out were some bits of stone.

If the twins had not been so sharp eyed they may well have ignored these stone chippings, but they noticed that some of them were coloured, they had been painted, and so the twins had a closer look at them.

There were quite a few bits of stone, so the twins treated them like a jigsaw puzzle and slowly pieced them together.

It seemed that whoever chipped the name off from the inscription stone had carelessly let them drop on to the floor and some, not many, but some had got brushed under the gap beneath the inscription stone.

The twins slowly put the stone chips together and then drew what they had, and it made part of a name;

After carefully examining it and checking it they realised that the largest picture was an owl which gave the letter 'M'.

Kepri was excited and said that she thought that they had seen something similar previously but hadn't thought it was significant, They rushed home to check it out.

When they found the old note book with the drawing in they knew that they had found most of the name;

possibly all of it.

The two of them, Kepri and Jabari carefully added the new pieces to their drawing and looked at it.

They discussed their drawing for a long time and eventually decided that they had all the information that they were liable to get. They also decided what to fill in where pieces were missing. Their teacher had told them about the first part of the name, the description, and MA'AT had said that it was correct. It was just the last letter of the name of which there was little left. After a lot of thought and a lot of looking through books about hieroglyphics, the twins decided what it must be. They drew the whole name up, filling in the missing parts.

They would now take this to MA'AT.

Kepri and Jabari stood in front of MA'AT. They were both excited and slightly frightened. What if they had got it wrong? Had they studied enough? If the name was wrong, even just one letter, they would have ceased the existence of a very nice goddess forever.

They handed MA'AT the piece of paper on which they had drawn the hieroglyphic name.

It seemed like ages passed, MA'AT looked and looked and looked at their drawing, looking at the name that the twins had handed to her.

Slowly the corners of MA'ATs mouth started to curl, and fortunately, curl upwards into a smile.

She looked to all those assembled in front of her and, with tears welling up in her eyes, she turned the piece of paper towards everyone and spoke, "We have a name" she said, and now we can speak it again.

MA'AT showed the name to everyone,

It was;

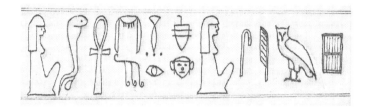

And the name is; 'SEMP' our beautiful queen of all festivities and fun.

It seemed as if the whole of their world was shaking, shaking with happiness as everyone chanted the name of their long lost 'SEMP'.

After a little while MA'AT calmed everyone down, and with a slightly more solemn expression said "Now we have to find her so that we can bring her back here, to us", and she looked towards Kepri and Jabari in hope.

4.

Kepri and Jabari sat with MA'AT and THOTH talking. They were trying to work out how to find SEMP.

It would have to be Kepri and Jabari as the body and spirit of SEMP had to still be in their world.

No one from the world of MA'AT and THOTH could cross over into it until SEMP had returned.

THOTH was the 'Keeper of records' amongst his many tasks and responsibilities and so they looked to him for any information he might have.

THOTH read from his book of records about the last time SEMP left their world and entered the world of the Pharaohs.

Shortly after SEMP crossed over she was followed by 𓀿𓆓𓎟𓂝𓏏 'she who's name cannot be spoken in words'.

There had always been disputes and animosity from 𓀿𓆓𓎟𓂝𓏏 'she who's name cannot be spoken in words' towards SEMP, and when 𓀿𓆓𓎟𓂝𓏏 'she whose name cannot be spoken in words' returned and SEMP didn't we questioned her about it. We asked her if she knew what had befallen SEMP, and whilst none from here can tell a lie while in our world, she remained silent, just smiling, but refusing to say anything.

This all occurred about 135 of your generations ago, around the time we call 'the great disturbance' in your world.

THOTH told Kepri and Jabari that was about all that was known, all that was recorded.

The only other information of any use was that they thought it happened somewhere close as it was here that the portal between the two worlds was sited.

After Kepri and Jabari returned to their own world they decided to visit the museum again and see if they could ask the person in charge some questions, so they visited the small museum in their town.

The person in charge was called a 'Curator' and she had to know a lot about the items that were there and about the history of Egypt.

Luckily the curator was happy to see them and even happier to talk with them as it was nice to find children who are interested in the subject that she loved.

The twins had worked out, using MA'ATs calculation of about four generations to equal one hundred years, that the 'great disturbance' was around the time of a Pharaoh called Akhenaten.

Now, most people have heard of Tutankhamun, Akhenaten was the Pharaoh before him and was probably Tutankhamun's father.

Akhenaten had changed his name from Amenhotep to Akhenaten after he became Pharaoh. He also decided that all the old gods of Egypt didn't exist and he dismissed all the priests and this was what caused the 'great disturbance'.

The twins were very interested in that period and they asked the curator all sorts of questions about what had happened.

The curator enjoyed talking with the twins and spent a lot of time discussing what she thought had occurred all those years ago, over three thousand and three hundred years ago.

It seems that the whole country was in a bit of a state, with much disturbance in the land and much distress. Even the twin's village was affected. Yes, apparently their village existed all of that time ago.

The twins asked about their village and the curator told them that it was much smaller then, but that it was important because it was near the site of the pyramids.

They asked what the village would have been like and the curator told them that it had been there a very long time. A long time before that period and had originally been just a few caves in the side of the hill which people had built out from.

Kepri and Jabari knew that their house backed onto the hillside and that it had been built out from caves a long long time ago. It had been handed down from generation to generation. It had been altered and rebuilt, enlarged and changed around, and the cave at the back had been blocked off a long time ago.

The twins thanked the curator of the museum before leaving to return home.

When Kepri and Jabari got home they went straight through to the back of their house, to where it joined onto the natural rock of the hillside.

They looked very carefully to see if they could find a way past where the cave had been blocked off many years ago.

Eventually they found a bit of wooden partition that was a little loose and they pulled it away just enough so that they could squeeze through.

Before they entered they made sure that their torches were working as it would be very dark in there.

The twins hadn't really known what to expect, but it seemed much larger in the cave than they had thought it might be.

Their torches lit up a small area and they followed the beam of light with their eyes as it picked out shapes of one kind and another.

Right at the back, where in ancient times the food had been kept as it would have been the coolest place, the torch beams picked out niches and shelves carved into the rock of the cave walls, and this is where food and other things would have been stored.

Just near the rear wall but slightly in front of it was what looked a bit like a table carved out of the rock. When the twins inspected it closer it looked as though a separate piece of stone had been stuck on top of it. Their torches picked out a black line all around the table just about a hand width below the top.

It looked as if the top piece had been stuck to the bottom using something like tar.

This 'table' looked interesting, but they were not sure what to do so they left the cave area to have a think about it all.

Kapri and Jabari returned to the museum and asked the curator about the stone 'table' which they had found in their cave. They described it as best they could and the curator said that it sounded like what the ancient people stored their grain in, such as corn, wheat or barley. She said that it was probably carved out to form a kind of box, but back in ancient times it would have had a wooden lid not a stone one.

This exited the twins because it meant that the 'table' most probably was hollow inside, and therefore might contain something of interest.

They rushed back home again and made their way through their home to the cave at the back.

By torchlight Kepri and Jabari carefully searched the ancient grain store. Centimetre by centimetre they checked to see if they could find any clue as to what might be hidden inside it.

As they searched along the back of it they found a patch of wax, almost unnoticeable, but on closer inspection, yes it was wax of some sort, probably bee's wax but with a lot of stone dust mixed into its surface to disguise it.

Carefully they picked at the wax, starting at the edges and slowly picking deeper into it.

After some time it began to feel as though something was beginning to come loose, was it a block of wax perhaps?

Gently they continued until the block of wax came free. Attached to the back of it was what looked like a papyrus scroll.

The twins quickly realised that they needed to be very careful and very gentle as it was probably very old and very delicate. One sudden jolt or slip and it might all crumble and be gone forever.

Although they didn't know what the papyrus scroll might say, the twins decided that it would be best to take it to MA'AT in the other world, and so they set off once more to see her.

MA'AT called for THOTH to deal with the scroll. THOTH was the right man for the job, he was the 'scribe', and he knew all there was to know about scrolls and papyrus and all things to do with writing.

He took the scroll and praised Kapri and Jabari for bringing it to him and for not damaging or destroying it.

THOTH then carefully, using various oils, potions and incantations unfurled the scroll and laid it out in front of both himself and MA'AT.

They both looked at it for some time before MA'AT invited THOTH to read it out loud.

"I am SEMP and these are my words, scribed by Rania and Sabra, siblings born on the same day"

After a short pause THOTH continued to read.

"I came to the land of the Pharaohs to try to make straight the Pharaoh in this time of great disturbance.

She whose name cannot be spoken in words had come to this place before me and beguiled the Pharaoh into believing that there was only one god, and that she was that god, giving herself the name of ATEN.

After I came to this land she whose name cannot be spoken in words followed me in order to stop my venture, and she attacked me.

We fought for many days and in many parts of the land until I had overcome her, captured her and bound her, I had her at my will.

It was then that she whose name cannot be spoken in words pleaded with me, she said that she would change and that she would put right all that she had done wrong and she pleaded that from then on she would only ever be good. She asked to be unbound by me.

I believed her words to be true and took her assurances to be honest, and so I unbound her and set her free.

It was when I had turned away and my back was towards her that she attacked and assaulted me and laid me low. She dealt me such blows that I was extremely weakened and unable to defend myself any more. She left me as dead.

If I had not been found by Rania and Sabra, and had they not taken pity on me and cared for me I would even now be no longer in existence.

As I lay weakened from the attack, she whose name cannot be spoken in words once more beguiled the Pharaoh and instructed him to have my name removed from every edifice, temple and tomb.

As each inscription of my name was

destroyed, so I became weaker and would eventually cease to exist, and were it not for Rania and Sabra I would surly no longer exist.

As I lay here weakening, they have been instructed by me to lay me into a grain store which will be my sarcophagus, and they should scribe my name inside it so that I will not completely cease to exist, and will remain until, with help, I can come back into the world".

MA'AT and THOTH went into a deep conversation, occasionally glancing at Kepri and Jabari, and then continuing their conversation.

Finally, after what seemed like a very long time, they turned to the twins.

THOTH spoke to them and said, "Thank you, you have found our beloved SEMP". He then looked towards MA'AT and back to the twins.

"We believe that you two were sent to us so that you could restore SEMP to her rightful place amongst us".

He continued, "We also believe that somehow you are connected to Rania and Sabra who first saved SEMP from she whose name cannot be spoken in words, and who placed her where you have found her, to keep her safe".

MA'AT now spoke, "We have one last task to ask you both to undertake. No one from our world can enter your world until SEMP is returned to us, and you cannot bring her here yourselves. THOTH believes he knows of a way that we can come together".

THOTH and MA'AT looked at each other again before MA'AT continued.

"We need you to make a map, a very accurate map of how you get from the cave where SEMP dwells to the inscription stone where you enter our world, but the map must be accurate so that we can retrace your steps in reverse in this, our world, if we are to succeed".

Kepri and Jabari agreed to this last task and returned to their world.

Kepri and Jabari thought very carefully, they had to make sure that their map was as accurate as it was possible to be,

They decided that the best way to measure the distances was to count how many steps it took to get from one place to the next. They realised that they could not walk in a straight line from their home to the pyramid, so they would have to think of a way that ensured that they didn't wander off a straight path or that they couldn't draw up properly.

Eventually they decided that they must only ever change directions like at a corner of a house, that is, square. Their teacher taught them that this was called a 'right angle' or '90 degrees', but they still had to work out how to do this and be exact, not a little less or a little more than 90 degrees.

They eventually found a way of doing this by using a piece of string with knots in it. They found a long piece of string and put a knot in after 3 measures, then another at 4 measures, and another at 5 measures. They then joined the string up, and when they pulled it so that each knot was at a corner it made a triangle, but not just any triangle, the string between the 3 and 4 lengths formed a perfect corner, 90 degrees, like this;

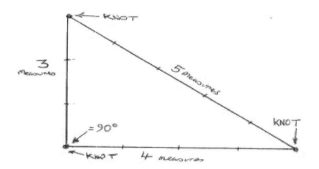

So they would be able to carry their right angle with them in their pocket and just pull it out when they needed it.

The map making was far more difficult than they had imagined it would be. Just getting from the cave at the back of their house to the front of it was not easy, it wasn't straight, they had to turn this way, then that way many times to get through different rooms and passages, just to get out of the house.

They made their way to the pyramid, counting how many steps they took from one point to the next, making a note of each turn and which way it was.

They repeated this many times to make sure that the steps they took were the same each time. They knew that if you get exited you may take bigger, longer steps, or if you walk slowly you may take shorter ones. They both knew that it was critical to get the distance right, so they keep walking between home and the pyramid until they were certain that they had drawn it accurately.

Their next problem was the pyramid itself. They had to climb about half way up the pyramid to get to the passageway entrance, each step was not the same as a normal step forward, none of the steps were the same size.

They turned again to string. They found another piece of string and used it to measure each step from front to back and then add it to the next measured step until they had as good a measurement as could be done.

After a lot of work the twins were satisfied that their map was as good as they could make it so they pressed themselves against the inscription stone at the end of the passageway in their favourite pyramid.

MA'AT, THOTH and ANUBIS were very pleased to see Kapri and Jabari when they reappeared, and even more so when the children showed them the map which they had made.

There was an excitement in the world of MA'AT, THOTH and ANUBIS that could be felt.

There were many others all gathering, all expectant, all hoping that the twins had made the map that could bring SEMP back to them.

THOTH told the twins that they now needed to 'walk the map' backwards from where they crossed from their world into this one, that would be how SEMP would be found, but only if they got it right.

It was Kapri who suggested that she and Jabari walked it separately to try to ensure that they were as close as possible.

Jabari went first, walking a distance, then turning this way and walking a little further, then turning again. He did this again and again until he had reached the end of his map.

Kepri then started her journey, walking, turning, walking and turning until she had reached the end of her walk.

Kepri and Jabari looked at each other and grinned. They were less than a couple of steps apart, so they knew that they had done well.

They looked around to see that they were in a beautiful garden. It had lotus blossoms, a very nice flower, and palm trees and fig trees, and all sorts of fragrances floating through the air. There was a little stream trickling its way through, and the garden was nice and cool, just the right temperature to make everyone feel comfortable.

"Are we in the right place?" the twins asked. They didn't expect anything like this, and they couldn't think that it was anywhere like the cave in which SEMP was laying.

"We really have to hope so" said MA'AT, "we only have this one chance to rescue her and bring her back to our world".

The twins, Kepri and Jabari looked around at the garden, it was perfect, there was nothing wrong with it, but were was SEMP?

How could she find her way to here, she was still inside the stone grain holder in the cave at the back of the twins house, and in the other world, and they, Kapri, Jabari, MA'AT, ANUBIS and THOTH were here in this garden in this world?

MA'AT must have read the twins minds and she took them to her side, she told them that THOTH knew many things and he would be able to bring SEMP here just as long as they had been accurate with their map.

THOTH stepped forward and began to make noises which the twins didn't recognise or understand, which were probably chants or songs of some sort.

He had all manner of things with him, candles were lit and sticks burned letting smoke wind its way upwards, and strange smelling incense wafted in the air.

THOTH walked from one place to another and made chants of some sort at each point where he stopped. He threw drops of water or something like water into the air and made mystical gestures with his hands and arms.

The twins watched along with everyone else, they dared not take their eyes from THOTH or what he was doing.

Before they realised what was happening the garden seemed to have other things appearing there. Slowly, it seemed, the cave began to emerge. Not to take over from the garden, not to replace it, but to merge with it so that both garden and cave were in the same space, and the stone grain store in which SEMP was laying became solid in front of them.

ANUBIS stepped forward to the stone tomb and with no effort what so ever, moved the stone lid as if it were as light as a feather.

A body lay inside, a beautiful woman, but she lay there very still, lifeless perhaps, but perfect!

Now MA'AT moved to the stone tomb where SEMP lay and from her robes brought out an 'Ankh' which looks a bit like a cross but with a loop at the top.

This was a very ancient symbol for 'life' and together with THOTH and ANUBIS they placed it on SEMPs lips while they all chanted.

Gently, softly, slowly SEMP opened her eyes and her lips parted, taking air into her body for the first time since she was laid in her sarcophagus all of those generations ago.

SEMP was alive!

She slowly sat up and was helped out of her sarcophagus to be once again amongst her own people, her friends.

SEMP looked around and when she saw the twins, went straight to them and said "Thank you Rania, and thank you Sabra, thank you for caring for me and for keeping your word to help me return to my world".

With that said she stood amongst her friends and the two worlds, that had for a moment in time been one, began to part, SEMP, ANUBIS, THOTH and MA'AT returning together to their world while the twins, Kapri and Jabari stayed in the cave, in their world.

All was now as it should be.

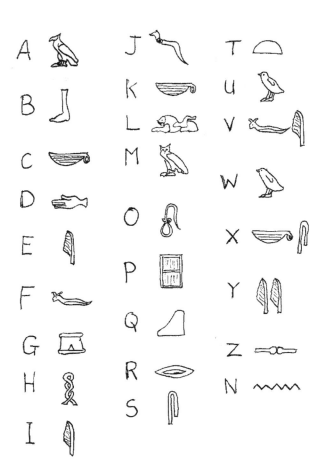

ANKH

Printed in Poland
by Amazon Fulfillment
Poland Sp. z o.o., Wrocław

63744426R00052